Mike Upchurch

Ben AND **Me**

Dorrance Publishing Co
585 Alpha Drive
Pittsburgh, PA 15238
Visit our website at www.dorrancebookstore.com

ISBN: 979-8-8860-4266-5
eISBN: 979-8-8860-4537-6

Ben AND Me

Dedicated to Beth.

Without her loving support this story would

only exist on my laptop.

Thank you, baby.

Chapter One

Thinking that I'd rather take a beating than go inside there, I had eased into Davidson's Funeral Home parking lot about an hour ago and just sat there in my truck with the air on for a minute. Allie couldn't get away from the office, Mom was coming later, so it was just me by myself. As I sat there, I looked down at my phone and saw the time and wondered if Ben would be coming into town for lunch that day, then caught myself as I realized how stupid a thought that was. My mind was filled with memories about Ben, and really, I didn't know what my reaction was going to be when I saw him in the casket. I had been to plenty of funerals, but this was somehow different. He wasn't even family, but honestly, he was closer to me than most of my family. Finally, deciding I couldn't put it off anymore, I climbed out of the truck and went in.

I saw a few folks I knew as I came in and nodded to them as I took off my hat. I found the room where they had put Ben and said hi to Ashley Biederman, who was standing outside in the hallway next to the doorway talking to some other ladies. Then I walked in as quietly as I could over to his casket. I'll tell you, I sure hated being there. Everyone was talking low and being all hush-hush, and it just gave me the creeps. I had stood there for a minute, looking at Ben lying there, and thought to myself how that really wasn't the man I knew. That man was a real cowboy; a man's man. I didn't know who this was in a blue suit and tie (Ben would have called it a "fancy banker's suit"). They even had his silver hair all slicked back, and he looked odd to me lying there without his hat. He'd be complaining about what they'd done to him getting him ready to be seen, that's for sure.

I guess I should introduce myself. I'm Mark Collins. I work at Union Ford Dealership here in town. Al Norris, my service writer, says

I'm the best tech he's got. But it's not because I know more, it's because I never complain and I just do my job. I credit that to Ben right there.

Anyways, I had taken off at lunch to come by and see Ben. I'm sitting here on this park bench now, thinking that some people ought to know some things better about my friend Ben if they didn't.

Chapter Two

I think back to when I first met Ben years ago. He was the kind of fella you had to work real hard to get to know, I'll say that for sure. He was about as quiet a man as you'd ever meet too.

Ben was one of the foremen for the Biederman Ranch out west of town, one of the biggest cattle ranches around. I had been hired on to work for them that summer, my junior year of high school. We were building new fences and repairing old fence lines most days. I was just a kid really, but I was strong for my age. Pops always worked me hard growing up, so I wasn't afraid of being on a ranch. I remember Pops and Mom looking at each other real strange though when I told them I would be working for Ben at that ranch.

Back then, Ben looked just like you'd think a ranch foreman should look; tall and lean with a tan and weathered face. He had a broom mustache but no beard on that square jawline of his. If you happened to get close to him in the early mornings, he smelled like a mixture of leather and ropes and Old Spice aftershave. Good, honest smells. He wore jeans that fit near perfect, yet they weren't new at all. His shirt was always tucked in proper, and he wore a big ol' belt buckle with a Texas star on it. I don't think he ever did rodeos though, just worked at the ranch. He wore a red bandana around his neck most days. He always wore a white cowboy hat that was perfectly creased and looked like it was supposed to be there. He never took that hat off much at all. And he always wore ropers. That's what they called the style of boots he wore. Nothing fancy, but he always kept them clean. To me, he always looked like he'd just stepped out of one of them Marlboro cigarette commercials we used to see in the old days.

Ben walked slow and measured but deliberate and carried himself with confidence, his back straight up. You always felt he knew exactly what to do every time he'd start out to do something. In a lot of ways, he was what I hoped to be like one day.

Anyways, Pops had dropped me off at the Biederman Ranch's main house that first day, and I saw Ben on the front porch talking to some of the other guys I knew who had also been hired on. You could tell he was the boss, as he sure looked the part standing over everyone else. I said hi to the others then walked up and stuck out my hand to Ben and told him my name.

He was reaching out to shake my hand, and before his hand made it all the way to mine, he stopped and said, "You Kate Collins' boy?"

"Yes sir," I said.

He went on and shook my hand real firm but stared at me a minute. I thought maybe he didn't like my mom at the time, the way he looked at me. They were about the same age. But anyways, I was glad to have a job and felt better when he told me to sign some paper he handed me.

Chapter Three

If I didn't say, I had been hired on that summer to try and earn enough money to buy Pops' old truck. It was an older, short wheelbase Chevy he kept parked out in the pole barn. He had bought a new truck a few years back and told me when I got old enough, he'd sell me his old truck. He said I'd appreciate it more if I had to work for it. He used it around the ranch rather than his new truck some days. It needed fresh paint, and it had a hole in the driver's side floorboard where you could see the road. The windshield was cracked all the way across, the cab smelled like a mixture of burnt engine oil and cigars, and the floor of the bed was some pretty weathered wood rather than steel with some boards missing, but I didn't much care. It was wheels, and that meant freedom! Besides, none of my buddies drove new trucks anyway.

I had figured I could make about fifteen hundred bucks working at the Biederman's before winter set in and I had to be back in school. Pops said he'd take about that much for the truck, so I was eager to work.

I worked for Ben all that summer except on the days it rained. Ben said we weren't working with a chance of lightning out there on the plains. I remember saying, "Good morning," to him just about every day when we'd meet up at the ranch house. Most days, I wouldn't get nothing but a look back or at the most a nod of the head. He was older than me, probably around 40, and I looked up to him. He was about the hardest working man I knew except for my own Pops.

Oh, I guess I should tell you, Pops was my Granddad. I didn't know my real dad. He was killed in a car wreck when I was three, and Pops let Mom and me live with him on his ranch. My grandma, who I never met, had passed on, so I think he liked having the company when he was home, and I know he liked having someone to cook for him for sure.

My mom's Christian name is Kathleen, but everyone around here calls her "Kate" or "Katie." Pops even called her "Katydid." Anyways, she was actually Pops' daughter-in-law. But Pops, not having a daughter of his own, he loved her like she was blood. Back in those days, Mom worked here in town at the West State Bank. You can see it from where I'm sitting here. She was always a pretty woman, I thought, and she'd just work then come home and cook for us and see to the housework and stuff. Just kept to herself mostly and didn't go out any. She loves to read, and it seemed like she was always curled up with a book, sometimes out on the swing on the front porch on days when it wasn't too cool. She never talked about my daddy, and I didn't ask much either.

Pops was like a dad to me, and I was pretty happy growing up. I loved Pops, for a fact. He was a good man, but in many ways, he was different from Ben. Well, he was older for one and didn't much care about his appearance like Ben did. He was a big man with a deep voice. Seemed like he always had on dark colored t-shirts with the sleeves cut off. He looked like a truck driver, which is what he was. He smoked cigars, and he would cough a lot, clearing his throat. Mom would say, "John, you make the house smell just awful," talking about those old cigars, and he'd just laugh. She always called him John, rather than Dad or Pops like I did. He had a bit of a beer belly, and his pants were always up under that belly a little, even though he wore suspenders. He always joked and said his chest had fell when talking about his belly.

As I said though, he was a good man, and he sure worked hard to make sure we had all we needed. None of us had to work Pops' ranch like a true ranch as some of the neighbors did. We didn't have no cattle or livestock of any kind, just the land that Pops inherited from his folks, my great-grandparents.

As I mentioned before, Pops was a trucker, and he owned an older longnose Kenworth with a sleeper. He had her dressed out pretty good with a big ol' polished visor across the windshield, and about a hundred running lights on it. It was what I would call candy red with a lot of stainless and polished aluminum on it, like the fuel tanks for example. You couldn't miss it when he was out on the highway. Even the stacks were chromed. It was a twin screw, and Pops had new rear fenders made for it out of polished aluminum when he started hauling for the quarry. I always got excited when I'd hear him pulling up to the ranch coming back from a run. He'd use that Jake brake, and you could hear him coming a ways off. Pops was loud, and his truck was too!

Pops said it was too hard to make a living ranching some years, so he drove his truck instead, like I said, hauling mostly for the Millerton Rock Quarry north of here. That was after being out on the road for years. That way, he'd be home nights. He took me out on the road with him sometimes when I was younger. His CB handle was "Sugar Bear," and he was always yakking on that CB radio. He had a big ol' laugh, and it seems like everybody on the CB knew Sugar Bear. I sure heard a lot of cussing on there, but he'd keep it turned down most of the time with me in there.

If we were making a run at night, sometimes I'd crawl up in the sleeper and stretch out, just listening to the different sounds of the highway and the different sounds coming from the truck. I could always tell when Pops was either slowing down to make a turn or was slowing down to stop, just by the gear changes. I used to count them when he'd take off too. His rig had what was called a hi-lo thirteen-speed tranny, and if he was fully loaded, he'd go through them all if he was getting out on the highway.

I always felt peaceful riding back there at night, just looking up through the sunroof in the headliner. Sometimes I would try to guess where we were by the turns or the stops. I loved being rocked to sleep by the moving of the cab and all the sounds I'd hear. I could always peek into the cab and look out the windshield to watch the highway if I got bored. Pops always had the radio on too. He would sing along with that bass voice of his sometimes. He sorta sounded like Johnny Cash. Pops used to say there were only two types of music: Country and Western! Those were good memories. I really felt safe and secure in that truck

I had to admit it seemed like a pretty cool life, but Pops said, "Son, get you an education. This ain't no life for a man." He said he'd pay for schooling if I'd go. Truth is, I think he said that because Mom told him she didn't want me traveling and being gone all the time. It would be too lonesome for her on that ranch with both of us gone.

So, anyways it was just me and Pops and Mom back then, and I'd help mow the fields or rake leaves or work on whatever needed fixing even when I was younger, but I never got paid. We all just did what had to be done, but I didn't ever have a paying job till that summer working for Ben.

Chapter Four

Anyways back to Ben. He sure worked us hard that summer, and he would even keep working while the rest of us would stop and take breaks. He was a lot stronger than us, of course. He'd work all day beside us and not talk much, except maybe to say just the minimum to get by with, telling us what to do. Sometimes we'd get spread pretty far apart, but we had two-way radios we could talk with. Ben kept two Igloo coolers in the bed of his truck filled with ice water, and we'd about drain them both before the day was out, as it got pretty hot and dusty out there on the plains. Ben didn't seem to mind the heat as much as us and didn't complain like we all did.

It seemed like at the time that Ben didn't like me at all, and I wasn't sure why back then. Some people just don't like other folks. Maybe he just didn't like the fact he was Ramrod to a bunch of kids instead of real cowboys like some of the other foremen. I would always try real hard to please Ben, just trying to get him to warm up to me. Not sure he ever did in those days. Anyways, we ran about twenty mile of fence that summer I reckon, and if Ben said six words to me other than telling me what to do, I'd be surprised.

There were four of us on the crew that summer, and we all knew each other from school. This town isn't all that big, and we only have one high school, so everybody knew everybody else. Larry Cobb was the only real cowboy among us, as he had done barrel racing since he was a kid. He was pretty good too. Danny Thompson and Jerry Robinson were the other two. Danny was the only one who had a license back then and kept his truck at the main house. He'd drop me off sometimes if I didn't have a ride. He had a pretty slick Z71 with a lift kit. We all got along real well, always trying to outwork each other.

When Ben had to run into town for supplies, naturally we'd talk about him. Jerry told us one day he'd heard how that Ben lost his wife and kid years back in some kind of accident and had lived alone since then. If only I'd known then what I know now, but I'll get to that.

When we'd take our lunch breaks, Ben would sit off to himself with Bandit and eat alone without saying nothing. We sorta felt sorry for him, but we just ignored his being quiet after a few weeks and went about our fence building, paying him no mind.

We'd work from about six each morning till around two in the afternoon, and then Ben would carry us back to the main house. Ben drove a big red Chevy Dually and pulled a twenty-foot open trailer that had all the fencing supplies on it. Around the ranch, we'd just ride on the trailer to get around. But when it was time to pack up for the day, he'd unhitch the trailer, and we'd all jump in the bed of Ben's truck to hit the highway.

I still remember how awesome it was feeling that cool wind on our faces, riding down the highway after being in that hot sun all day. Ben's truck had the big block 454 in it, and he'd get that old truck really moving getting back to the main house, and that was about the best part of the day for us. Sometimes I think he drove fast just to hurry and get rid of us though.

Bandit always rode up front with Ben in the cab. No one else was allowed in that front passenger seat, I reckon. Oh, Bandit was his dog, a Blue Heeler. A pretty smart dog really with the most beautiful blue eyes—for a dog, anyways. He didn't leave Ben's side much that I remember. He'd watch us work, but he was as faithful a dog as a man could want, never running off far and would come running when Ben would whistle. Ben never used Bandit to work the cows that I remember, but I reckon he could have though.

Chapter Five

Well, I worked all that summer as I said, and between having to buy clothes or lunches or some other things I wanted, I ate into my money saved up, and I came up a little short on having the whole amount of money for the truck. I was embarrassed to approach Pops, but I finally told him I only had about twelve hundred saved up, and I could work some more in town for the rest if he'd wait.

"Son, don't worry about it," he told me. "You can have the truck for a thousand. Your Momma already told me you didn't have it all, and I don't need the money to eat on anyway. I know you've worked hard, and it's not like it's brand new. Besides, you'll need some cash to fix it up."

I was glad to have that truck and spent a lot of time working on it even before I got my license, trying to make it better. I had gotten some tongue and groove oak flooring from the building salvage store out on the bypass and had stained them and made a new bed floor. It looked pretty good really, and then I didn't have to worry about things falling through anymore. The engine and tranny in the truck were good and didn't need anything done to them. It was mostly cosmetics that I worked on. I had a new front glass put in, and I had added a pretty good stereo a friend had gave me. Pops even sprung for a new set of tires for me that Christmas.

When I graduated from high school the next year, I ended up going off to college in that old truck, like I promised Mom I would. Well, it wasn't college really, just an automotive trade school about three hours away, but I was looking forward to learning how to work on cars and my truck too. I would come home from school when I could. Now and then, I might see Ben out on the highway or in town in his Dually. I would wave to him, but we never talked.

That was a two-year trade school I was in, and that second year, I came home for spring break. When I pulled up to the house, I was surprised to see Ben's red Dually parked in front that day. I said hey to Bandit in the front seat of the cab, scratching him behind the ears, and walked up the front steps and into the house. The house felt nice and cool with both the front and back doors open. We had screen doors, of course, but Pops liked the fresh air, so the doors stayed open a lot. Fact is, we don't have hard winters here.

Anyways, I had looked around, but there wasn't anyone there. Then I looked out the kitchen window, and there sat Pops and Ben at the picnic table under our big oak tree, and they were facing each other. Pops was chewing on that ever-present cigar in his mouth, and they were talking. It was always funny to me how Pops would use his hands as he talked, and they were moving pretty good out there. I figured he couldn't say anything at all if you ever tied his hands up.

I wasn't sure if I should go out there, but heck, I felt I had as much right as anyone to be amongst them. It was my house too, after all! So, I headed out the screen door and strolled up to them and said, "Hey."

Pops looked at me and said, "Hey son, you home?"

Ben looked up but didn't say anything, then turned to Pops and said, "So, it's a deal then? I appreciate the work," and got up to leave.

Pops shook Ben's hand goodbye, then turned his attention to me, asking how it was going at school. I said it was going okay, then asked what Ben was doing there, after he'd gotten out of earshot.

"Oh," Pops answered, "he's going to tear down that old shed over there for me. I want him to build a new pole barn for the tractor and stuff, and that's about the best place really, 'cuz that way I won't have to make a new driveway."

"Well, how come you hired him?" I asked, reminding him I could help him do it, and it wouldn't cost anything.

"Well, I'm getting to old to work that hard anymore" he laughed, and then he said, "Besides, we owe Benny in a way I reckon, and I don't mind giving him some work."

"We owe him?" I asked, surprised. "First I heard of that!" I exclaimed.

"Well..." Pops said, and then stopped, looking off in the distance. He took his cigar out of his mouth and thought for a minute. Then he took a long breath and said, "I reckon it's time you knew the truth, son," picking bits of tobacco off his lips while he spit out small pieces now and then as he talked.

He went on, "I was hoping your mom would tell you one day, but she has avoided it all these years like we both have. Sit down here." He motioned, pointing to the picnic table.

What in the world….? I thought to myself as I sat down. I sure didn't like the look on Pops' face, serious and all.

Chapter Six

"You see, son" Pops began as we sat there at the picnic table that day, "I'm not sure you knew this, but Benny's wife and son were killed years ago out on Highway 162 in a head on crash. Well sir, they were killed by a drunk driver." He paused for a minute, looking off, then he went on. "That wreck killed the drunk driver too, and that driver was your daddy."

As I stared at him in disbelief, he continued on rather slowly and softly, his eyes kinda wet.

"Your dad had been in town that night and had too much to drink at the bar he was at, over at Linda's Place. Instead of getting a ride or calling me and leaving his truck there like he shoulda, he drove off toward his house. Out there on 162, he crossed over into the other lane and hit Barbara, Benny's wife, head on, and they was all killed instantly. I seen Benny at the scene that night after the Highway Patrol called Katie, and she called me, and he wouldn't even look at me. I guess it was the most horrible thing I'd ever seen, and there wasn't anything I could say to Benny 'cept how sorry I was. He hadn't really said much to any of us since that day, so I figured asking him to build the barn might ease things a bit."

Now it all began to make sense. Maybe Ben blamed me in a way for what happened to his family. I was alive, and his wife and son weren't, and him having to look at me was a reminder every day of what had been taken from him.

Pops went back in the house, and I just sat there at the picnic table that day, and I was numb. I sat in silence, looking off, trying to process what I had heard. Now I also understood why Mom would get so mad when I said I wanted to go into town and drink beer with the other guys on Friday nights. After I had turned 18, there wasn't much she could do, but she hated it, and now I knew why. She always made me promise to get a ride home if I had too much to drink.

Well sir, I knew now why Ben hated me, or thought I did anyways. I had a new respect for the man too. I thought to myself that he was a good man who just kept quiet and worked, not bothering nobody and keeping all that grief inside him all those years.

I told Mom that night when she got in from work that I knew about Daddy and what had happened, and that Pops had told me everything. I also apologized for drinking too and said that I would never do that to her, be so drunk that I would still drive. We cried together a bit, then I hugged her and went back to my room, just feeling sick inside. I was sick that my daddy had done what he did, sick that Ben held it against me, and sick that my family kept the truth from me too. I remember thinking that night that I would avoid Ben the rest of my life if I could, 'cuz I didn't even know what to say to him.

Chapter Seven

I finished up automotive school at the end of May that year. After graduating, I hung around the next day to pack up. After I finished loading all my stuff in the back of my truck, I headed back home for good. As I finally pulled in the driveway back at the house, I saw Ben's red Dually out back.

"Crap!" I said, out loud as I hit the steering wheel. Now, there wasn't any way to avoid him unless I hid in the house till he left, but I knew that wasn't the right thing to do. I needed to confront him. I needed to let him know that I knew what happened and how sorry I was. Pops must have been out making a run, and Mom was still at work, so it was just me and him.

So I walked in the house and set my backpack down on the kitchen table. My mouth was now as dry as could be thinking about talking to Ben. I felt like it was so dry that if I coughed, dust might come out, so I got a drink of water from the sink. Mustering up all the courage I could, I walked out the back screen door and headed toward Ben, who was up on a ladder putting screws in the metal roofing. Bandit was by the base of the ladder and rose up when saw me, expecting a rub, which I obliged.

I really wasn't even sure what I was going to say to him. I had a feeling he wasn't wanting to hear anything I had to say, but I really wanted to just tell him I knew what had happened and that I was sorry, and that I wished it hadn't all happened like it did. I was hoping he'd say that it was okay, but honestly I didn't think that was likely. So with a pretty big knot in my stomach, I stood at the ladder and looked up at Ben.

"How's it coming?" I asked, just trying to get the ball rolling with small talk.

Ben glanced down, saw it was me, and kept working. He was

sweating pretty good, and I could tell he was tired, and now I was feeling like a fool for even saying anything to him at all.

"Do you need some help?" I asked, knowing he'd probably say no.

"Naw, I'm 'bout done for the day," he answered matter-of-factly.

Well, I then had a choice; I could wait till he came down off the ladder and talk to him about the wreck, or I could go back in the house and pray I never had to see him again. I chose to stay till he came down and then try to make amends. Ben finally came down the ladder, and I backed off giving him room.

"It looks great so far," I said, looking up at the roof of the barn.

Ben walked away headed to his truck, so I followed him.

"Ben" I said, when he stopped at his tool box sitting on the tailgate. "I need to tell you something. I wanted to tell you that I know about my daddy killing your wife and boy," I kept on, not giving him a chance to say anything back. "I didn't learn that till a couple of months ago, and I just wanted to tell you how sorry I was."

I realized I sounded pretty nervous and hoped he couldn't tell. I kept eye contact with him though, which is what Pops had always said I should do when talking to someone. He looked at me for a minute, then finished putting his tools away and closed the tailgate. He looked back at me like Clint Eastwood would look in the movies sometimes, when he'd squint his eyes at bad guys in them old Westerns before he would shoot them dead.

Ben came around and leaned over the bed of his truck and looked down into the bed for a minute, like he was thinking.

"You didn't know about the wreck?" he finally said, looking back up at me.

"No sir," I replied. "They told me Daddy died in a car wreck, but they never told me he was drunk and that other people died. They never talked about him really. I don't remember him, and I guess they thought it was best to let me always think he was a good man."

Ben looked off across the bed of his truck, and out into the field.

He finally said, "Mark," and paused. I think that may have been the first time he had ever called me by my name, usually it was just "kid." Anyways, he looked back to me, and he said "Your dad WAS a good man. Jimmy and I was best friends. There's more about that night of the wreck than you know, though. I always figured you knew about your dad and the wreck, but there's more to it. I didn't much want to be around you when you worked for me back a few years ago, because of what you reminded me of. And it wasn't just losing my wife and my boy. It was that whole awful night. But you deserve to know the truth."

Ben looked out across the field again. He was leaned up against the bed of his truck with his elbows on the bed rail and his hands folded with his leather work gloves still on, those kind he always wore that were sorta orangey-yellow in color. Anyways, he didn't say nothing for a minute.

Then he sighed, straightened up, and took his gloves off. He took a big swig of water from a water bottle, swished it around in his mouth, and spit it out on the ground. Then he looked over at me again, like he was gathering up what to say.

Chapter Eight

After what seemed like forever that afternoon, he said, "The truth is your dad and me was both drinking that Friday night. But he'd had more and was pretty lit, more so than me. Your dad asked me to drive him home, but I said that I wanted to stay and play pool some more, and that he'd be fine if he drove himself home. He kept on, but I refused and said no, that I was staying in the bar and that he needed to man up and quit being a wimp. I told him he didn't have that far to drive, and he'd be okay. Then he left out of the bar and got in his own truck to leave."

Ben paused for a minute. He cleared his throat, looked back out across the field, then continued.

"The truth is I've wished a million times I had drove him home that night. I was still shooting pool when Earl the bartender told me I had a phone call and to take it in the back office. It was Barb's sister Jean. Frank Jacobs, the chief of police, had called her because I wasn't at home, and they couldn't get in touch with me. She told me what had happened. I sat back there in the office in shock for quite a while. Not knowing what else to do, I gathered myself up and finally drove out to the wreck on the highway.

By the time I got there, they'd already taken everybody away by ambulance. I saw your granddad standing there, looking into Jimmy's truck, and I couldn't come up with the courage to tell him that Jimmy asked me to take him home that night, and I refused. To be honest, I wasn't sure what his reaction would be. He had a reputation for fighting back then, and he was a lot bigger than me, and I guess I was afraid of what he might do.

Anyway, I just stood there looking out into the night, as cold and lonely and broken as I'd ever felt. Barb and Ryan would still be alive if I had driven him home, and Jimmy would be too." He looked back to me again and, with a sigh, said, "Truth is, I never told anyone about all this before today. Who could I tell? I kept it in me and figured I'd go to my grave with it."

He stopped again for a minute, just looking off.

"I'm kinda glad to finally get it off my chest to be honest though. I shoulda called your grandad that next day, but I was just too ashamed and too afraid, knowing Jimmy would still be alive if it weren't for me. I have asked the sweet Lord Jesus to forgive me for that and more probably a thousand times, and I hope you can forgive me too, Mark."

I looked at Ben. I saw he had true sorrow in his eyes that were now watery. I nodded my head, fighting back my own tears, and told him that I had come to him to ask for HIS forgiveness that day, and of course I could forgive him.

I rubbed Bandit on the head for a minute, who'd come over between us, just pondering what I'd heard. Then I looked out across the field and said, "Man, you kept that bottled up in you all those years? That must have really been hard, Ben."

"I live with it about every day," he answered. "I'm the reason everybody died that night. It might as well have been me plowing into Barb's car. I couldn't really look at you much on the ranch back then and talk to you because working with you every day was a horrible reminder for me of what I'd done. You know, you really favor your dad. You look kinda like he did when we was in school. I didn't want to be around you, but I couldn't tell you why, so I just kept to myself. I guess the worst of it is, I know I need to tell your grandpa and Kate the truth too. Will you stay around here while I do that?"

"Of course, Ben" I said.

After a few minutes of quiet, I told him, "I want you to know, Ben, that I'm just sorry you had to live with that pain all this time. I never knew my daddy, and I don't hold it against you that he's gone. You weren't driving; he was. You know, all us guys at the ranch wondered why you was so quiet, and just figured you was mad at God or something 'cuz you lost your family. None of us knew that you blamed yourself for them being gone."

Looking back, I don't suppose there was ever a harder thing a man had to do than for Ben to tell Pops and Mom what really happened. But he did. He manned up and told them both right there at our kitchen table that night. I watched Pops' face as Ben talked, not sure what to expect.

But the first thing Pops said was, "Benny, I wished you'd told me that night. You can't be blaming yourself, son. Jimmy knew he could have called me."

There were a lot of tears shed around that table, and there were hugs, and there was forgiveness, and there was healing that night too. Healing that had needed to take place for years. I do remember something Mom said to Ben that night though that I don't reckon I'll ever forget.

She said, with tears streaming down her face, "Ben, you didn't make Jimmy drink that night. He got drunk just about every Friday night, and other nights too. We argued about his going out and drinking all the time. I knew he was going to kill himself if he didn't stop. You need to stop blaming yourself. I'm just so sorry it was your family it happened to."

They all hugged again, and we all said goodnight to Ben as he left.

Chapter Nine

Ben finished up the barn for Pops that next week, and I helped since I was home. We all stayed in touch after that. When I'd see Ben in town, we'd always talk. I would meet him for lunch over at Smokey's Bar-B-Que some days when he had time. He wouldn't say much as we ate, but it was just real comfortable being with him. I would actually get him to laugh by telling about some stupid thing that happened at work. Well, it was more a chuckle than a laugh, but just seeing him smile did me good.

Sometimes I'd go out to the ranch on Saturdays, and I might find him out in the fields. We'd sit out on the tailgate of his truck and just talk. I wanted to know more about my daddy, and he told me a lot that I didn't know. Good stuff too. Like how he could shoot pool better than about anybody, and how he was always happy with a lot of friends. And he played on the school baseball team and was pretty good too. Ben said Daddy was popular in school and was really out-going, and he had a real quick smile. Ben said he himself was always quiet and shy, especially around girls.

I remember one spring, Ben asked if I had ever shot a rifle. I told him no, that Pops never hunted or fished, so naturally I never learned. Ben had a rifle he kept in a gun rack in the back of his truck. I think it was for varmints mostly, like coyotes. It was a .30/30 Winchester, and he looked at it with pride when he took it out that day. He said, "This here's a Henry," adding that it was the finest rifle ever made. I couldn't believe how loud that thing was the first time I pulled the trigger! I also couldn't believe how far I missed the bottle he'd set up. He actually laughed out loud with a "Hah!" at that.

Then he set up one of those potato chip cans and asked where I wanted the round to go. He didn't call them bullets; he said they were rounds.

"Dot that letter 'i,'" I dared, which he did.

He had steady hands, I'll say that. We would "plink" now and then, as he called it, shooting cans and bottles and stuff. I got to be a pretty good shot later on with Ben teaching me, but not as good as him. I was pretty sure there wasn't anything Ben couldn't do and do well.

Ben had a lot of wisdom about a lot of different things. He'd been in the service, but he never talked about it. Only reason I knew is because he had a picture of himself in his uniform on the mantel of his fireplace.

Ben taught me a lot of things. He taught me how to fell a tree with a chainsaw, so it'd fall where you wanted. He showed me how if you were painting something, if you found the "grain" of it, then it wouldn't leave brush marks. He tried to show me how to use a lasso one day, but I never got the hang of it. He even taught me that peanut butter could remove chewing gum from a dog's hair, but I'd like to pretty much forget about that day. Let's just say Bandit kept his distance from me for a while after that.

I was able to teach Ben one thing though. He watched one afternoon as I rebuilt the carburetor on his truck. He stood there looking over my every move, absorbing it all, asking questions. That was Ben; a good teacher, but a good student too. It wasn't all that hard to rebuild it really; it was just a four barrel Rochester, but I didn't know if he knew that. So I was hoping he might be impressed with my mechanical skills. I took my time and made extra sure it was going to be perfect.

After I finished up, I bolted the carb back on the engine and told Ben to fire it up. I adjusted the idle mixtures screws and got it purring like a kitten. There weren't any leaks, and when he came around to the front of the truck, he was smiling pretty big. He looked at me and said, "That's a damn fine job, Mark."

I grinned back and said, "Well, now YOU know how to do it the next time."

He shoved two twenties in my shirt pocket and smiled and said, "If you did it right, there shouldn't be no next time. It ought to outlast me."

I didn't know he'd be right.

Chapter Ten

Ben never remarried, and I think he was happier that way. He lived alone in a bunkhouse on the Biederman ranch, not too far off the highway. I would take him some of Mom's cooking some evenings, and we'd sit out on his porch and eat together. He said he really enjoyed her cooking. Bandit had to have his share of scraps too, of course. Sometimes I'd luck up when Ben would grill steaks and call me over. You couldn't get fresher or better meat than from the Biederman's own cows there on the ranch, I reckon.

Ben wasn't a real religious man, and by that, I mean he didn't go around preaching, carrying a Bible, and trying to convert others. But he had a deep faith. He'd talk about God now and then, how his life changed after the wreck, and how God had been good to him. I do remember that back when I worked for him on the ranch, before he ate his lunch, he always bent his head over for a minute. Ben went to a little cowboy church out near Cloverdale's but never asked me to go with him. But that was Ben, just keeping to himself and figuring if I ever wanted to go, I'd bring it up. Allie and me have our own church anyways; we go to the First Baptist Church here in town. Just about everybody we know goes there, and we enjoy it.

Now, when I was hanging around Ben all that time, I wasn't looking for him to try and replace my daddy. I just always liked being with him, and I hoped he felt the same. He did like being alone though, you could tell. When I'd overstayed my welcome some days, he'd say something like, "Well you can stay out here on the porch, but I'm going in. I'll see ya."

In the wintertime, some evenings I'd drive out to the bunkhouse, and we'd just sit, watching a crackling fire Ben had built in the fireplace. Me, Ben, and Bandit, just looking into the fire and not saying much for quite a while. Around Christmas, Ben would put up a small tree. He had ornaments his son Ryan had made hung on there. It really made me sad to see those.

Sometimes he would light Christmas candles too, and we'd sit there in the dark just staring into the fire. It was neat to see the shadows dancing around the room that the flames made. Then Ben would yawn and that would make Bandit yawn, and I knew those were my cues to head out.

He stopped by the house one day, which I'd almost forgot about till just now, and said his truck was starting to make a noise in the rear end and could I take a look at it. I rode with him down the road, sitting in the back with Bandit up front. As soon as I heard it I knew it was the pinion bearing. I told him I could fix it, and I wouldn't charge him anything. He wheeled around without smiling and said, "You'll do no such thing. I always pay my way."

But that was Ben too. He was prideful, Pops would say about him. Didn't want no handouts, nor people doing favors for him. It was the way men like him grew up.

"You don't be owing anybody but the Lord if you can help it, Mark," he told me one time.

Chapter Eleven

As I sit here today, I realize a lot sure has changed. Pops died a while back. He had gotten up in years, but it still hurt to lose him. He didn't get around very good toward the end, as he'd had a stroke. I hated seeing him suffer, not being able to do as much as he was used to. He'd just sit out there on the front porch and doze off. We had arranged for a woman we knew to move in and care for Pops. He had to quit driving after the stroke and depended on her and the rest of us to get around, and that sure made him ornery. He was stubborn anyway and wouldn't do like the doctor said about eating right and wouldn't stop smoking them cigars either, right to the end.

When Pops passed, the ranch went to Probate. He had a pretty good stack of medical bills and a loan on the ranch we didn't know about that had to be paid off. I think it was to overhaul his truck or maybe it was to pay taxes, I'm not sure. Might even have been to pay for my schooling. Anyways, after everything was paid off, the ranch was sold off, and me and Mom split what was left. That was in the will Pops left. We sold his rig to a trucker friend of his and probably got less than it was worth, but we knew he'd take care of it. Mom had gotten married a few years back to Will Crawford, my stepdad. Will had a house just to the east a ways, so they live there. He's a good man and takes really good care of Mom. He works for the state as an inspector and makes a good living. Allie and me see them pretty regular.

I had asked Mom one day why she never hooked up with Ben. She told me he just never seemed all that interested in her.

"Besides he's not really my type," she said. "It would drive me crazy to be around a man who never talked!" she laughed. I had imagined having Ben for a dad before, but I guess it would have changed things a lot, so it was better they didn't marry, I reckon.

Oh, and I got married to Allison Kincaid from over Dallas way.

She moved here when her dad got transferred with the pipeline. Allie and me hit it right off when we met. I had gotten a job right out of school at the Union Ford Dealership here in town. I can't remember if I mentioned that or not.

Anyway, Allie had brought her Mustang in to get it serviced, and I was "smitten," as Ben used to say, by her looks. Sometimes I think the only reason she married me was to keep her ol' beater of a car running. It's not the GT, and it has the V6 engine, but it's been a good car. She needs a new one, but she says we need to pay off my truck first. I bought a new F-150 from the dealership before we ever met. It was pretty pricey even though I got a good deal as an employee, but I took out the loan down at Mom's bank, which helped some. Allie's really good with money, more so than me, so it won't be long till it's paid off.

I took Allie around to Ben after we met, and I could tell he approved. I knew she liked him a lot too. From then on, it was usually Allie and me hanging out with Ben. The three of us playing Monopoly was always a hoot because when Ben won, we'd both act like we were frustrated at him. We didn't really care though. I think we wanted him to win, really.

Sometimes Allie would pick up a bottle of wine, not the real expensive kind, but we would all sit there and drink wine out of Ben's mason jars. Allie would burst out laughing when Ben would stick his little pinkie out while sipping, pretending he was high class. Actually, he WAS pretty high class to me. Allie said the reason he was always so neat and fussy about the way things looked was because he had OCD. She would laugh and say, "He even creases his jeans!"

I defended him saying that was just for church! I think he was neat like he was because he was in the military, but he was a neat freak for sure, like my Mom.

Bandit would always lay by Allie when she was around. Only time he chose someone over Ben I think. Did I mention that Bandit got down in his hind legs, and Ben had him put to sleep? Buried him out behind the bunkhouse. That was a sad deal right there. Ben said he reckoned Bandit was around 14 years old. I offered to get Ben another pup, but he said no, that he didn't want another mouth to feed. Truth is, I don't think he could stand the hurt of losing another dog.

Chapter Twelve

Well, I don't think I've left out much. The way I found out about Ben was Mom had called me Tuesday morning to tell me that he'd had a major heart attack out on the ranch. She said they had life-flighted him by helicopter to the hospital the next town over, but they couldn't revive him. She had found out from Ms. Shelley at the bank, whose daughter is married to Kenny Biederman. It hit me pretty hard. Harder than I thought it would. And all those memories of Ben and me were brought back to me today as I sit here, and that was pretty tough to walk through in my mind.

I saw on the marquee when I came in where Ben's full name was Abraham Benjamin Willis. A good, solid Bible name. I guess he didn't want to be called Abe though. Truth is "Ben" seemed to fit him just fine. Pops called him "Benny" from all the way back in the day when him and Daddy hung out, but I don't think anyone else did.

Before I had left the room, I leaned over and kinda quietly said, "Rest easy now, Ben," as I patted his cold hand. "You've earned it," I said. "If ever there was a man that deserved to be let in to the Good Lord's Paradise, it's you my friend. I'm sure you're enjoying being with your family again, and say hi to Daddy and Pops for me."

Then I had walked outside into the sunshine, wiping a couple of tears away. I just stood there in the parking lot for a minute. Then I took in a big breath of air and blew it out with a sigh. I walked across the street to this park and sat down on this bench. Normally, I would have gone right back to work after stopping by to pay my respects with someone passing. But not today. This time, I called back to the dealership and asked for Al and told him I was taking the afternoon off.

I just wanted to be alone, thinking back to Ben and me. Just now, thinking about work, I was reminded that these days I call an engine in a car an engine and not a motor because of Ben. I'm about the only one that does at the dealership. They all say "motor." They're just a bunch of hicks, I reckon.

"What size motor's in it?" they'd say if they was looking at a hot car.

"A motor is electrical, and if it runs on internal combustion, it's an engine," Ben would always remind me when I called the 454 in his truck a motor.

"Your motor runs pretty good," I'd say, wincing as soon as I did, knowing I was about to get lectured. Guess I'm just a hick too, but I reckon he finally got through to me though about calling it an engine.

I say a lot of other things different because of him too. He had a pretty big influence on me. I guess it's really true that good guys always wear a white hat. Ben was a good man. A good, godly man.

Epilogue

Well, maybe I'll go home and mow the grass before Ben's funeral this evening. It's getting pretty high with the rain we've had of late. Ben would have shaken his head when he saw it high like it is. He'd just look at me, knowing that look would have shamed me for not keeping it looking better. He was that way about all he owned. The grass in front of his bunkhouse was cut each week, his truck was washed about every Sunday, and he kept the interior clean; his front porch was swept off pretty regular, and the inside of his house was kept straight.

"A man takes care of the things the Good Lord's trusted him with," he would always say.

I guess I owe him for how I turned out in a lot of ways. No, I'm not a rancher like him, and I don't wear cowboy clothes like he did, mainly because I wear my mechanic's uniform every day. But I try to keep to myself and respect other people's stuff. I pray some when its quiet, and I work hard like Ben did. I still like the smell of Old Spice, but Allie doesn't, so I don't wear it. She likes that other cologne I can't think of. It has some kind of French name.

Man, I miss Ben a bunch already. Well, I'd best get to it. Thanks for listening to me rattle on. I wish you'd met Ben. You'd have loved him too. You know, I don't know that I ever said I loved him to his face. Maybe he knew it though. I hope he did.

Well, take care. I need to get going. Mark here, signing off. Y'all be careful.

The End